the 4th Magi

by Stephen Elisha

THE KINGMAKER'S QUEST: BOOK ONE – THE 4TH MAGI ©
www.stephenelisha.com

ISBN- 978-0-9842177-5-5
ISBN-10 0-9842177-5-4

Copyright © 2010 by Stephen Elisha
Interior maps © 2010 by Joyce Sloan
Book cover design & Interior design © 2010 by Nathan Fisher,
www.nathanfisher.net
Publishing and marketing support provided by:
Jeff Pederson at JPED Publishing Group, www.jpedpublishing.com

Library of Congress Cataloging-in-Publication Data
Elisha, Stephen
The Kingmaker's Quest: Book One – The 4th Magi

Printed in the United States of America
2010—First Edition

Table Of Contents

Preface

This inspiration for this story came in the form of two separate sources: my time spent in the Middle East, and the research of Fredrick "Rick" Larsen, an intellectual property and business law professor at College Station, TX. My first visit to Saudi Arabia was as a soldier in Operation Desert Storm, where I first began to ponder the events leading up to the familiar Christmas story and, more importantly, the journey of the Wise Men or Magi.

In December of 1990 I found myself in Dammam, Saudi Arabia, with the 1st Infantry Division waiting for an Iraqi attack that never came. I wondered whether the Magi might have come from that part of the world, and if so, what did they see that prompted them to make their way to Jerusalem. Furthermore, I wondered why they posed the question to Herod, *"Where is He who is born King of the Jews? For we have seen His star in the east and have come to worship Him."* My curiosity extended to Herod's response as recorded in the gospel of Matthew, *"When King Herod heard about this, he was very upset, and so was everyone else in Jerusalem."* This last sentence jumped out at me. This did not sound at all like the picture portrayed in countless Christmas cards showing three men on camels following a laser beam-like light illuminating their path across the desert.

Why hadn't anyone else seen 'the star'? If it was like what is depicted in the Christmas cards, then surely there should have been a parade of people from around the world descending on Jerusalem as they followed "yonder star." Instead, it seemed as though neither Herod, nor anyone else in Jerusalem knew anything about what the Magi were referring to.

It wasn't until the fall of 2007 that I came across Rick Larsen's compelling presentation of The Star of Bethlehem *(www.bethlehemstar.net)* that I found answers to the questions I had regarding the story of the Magi. I had already started writing The 4th Magi as a story for my children, but now I had scientific and historical evidence that provided the necessary authenticity for the story. Rick Larsen's website and his DVD, The Star of Bethlehem, were fundamental to my understanding of this portion of history, and played an important role in the formation of the narrative that will unfold throughout the following pages.

My hope is that this story will bring to life the message of Christmas and encourage you to stand at the crossroads and, like the Magi, look, ask about the ancient paths, where the good way is, walk in it, and find rest for your soul (Jeremiah 6:16).

Note to the reader:

This book uses the modern names for stars, planets, and other astronomical terms. The conversational style and vocabulary are also modernized, so the reader can simply enjoy the story as it unfolds, without needing to step outside of the narrative to look up an ancient name or obscure term.

Let your adventure begin, as you journey with The 4th Magi on his trip to an exotic destination – and an eternal destiny!

the 4th Magi

1

It's hard to say when the adventure really began. If you ask me, I would say it slowly unfolded over a number of months, and then peaked with the most remarkable trip I have ever taken.

My name is Arcturus, and I am a Magi. Well, actually I am an apprentice Magi. I was raised in the School of the Magi in Persepolis during the reign of Phraataces, son of Phraates IV. I was orphaned at the age of two and brought here to learn the ways of the Wise Ones. It was Milan who took me under his wing and raised me as his own. He was the Magus from the port city of Siraf and a descendant of the Jews, and of The Immortals, the fiercest of Parthian warriors He was also the Rab-Mag, or the Chief of the Magi.

The Magi were wise in the ways of the stars. They devoted their lives to studying the heavens; they had kept meticulous records of the skies for hundreds of years. They also were advisors to the king and helped administer the empire. All of these details keep me from telling the story, which I am so anxious to tell.

Milan's eyes were not as sharp as they used to be, but mine were sharp and keen. He relied on me to tell him the position of the stars. I knew all the constellations, but I didn't know how to read them. So, I would tell him if Cassiopeia lay low in the southern sky or if the Pleiades were at zenith. I would also tell him the position of the wandering stars, something he was very interested in. He would always say, "Yes, yes, but I'm looking for the sign." Every night I would ask "What sign is it you seek, Rab-Mag?" And he would say "The sign of the promise." But he would never tell me more than that.

Milan was convinced that the heavens were key to understanding the times, often quoting the ancient prophet, *"The heavens declare the glory of God; the skies proclaim the work of his hands. Day after day they pour forth speech; night after night they display knowledge. There is no speech or language where their voice is not heard. Their voice goes out into all the earth, their words to the ends of the world. In the heavens he has pitched a tent for the sun, which is like a bridegroom coming forth from his pavilion, like a champion rejoicing to run his course. It rises from one end of the heavens and makes its circuit to the other; nothing is hidden from its heat."*[1] And then he would follow the quote with "Perhaps the heavens will reveal the sign tonight."

In the eighth month of the first year of Phraataces' reign the wandering star Jupiter was in the zodiac of Leo. It was behaving rather oddly, in a manner I had never seen before. As it moved through Leo it seemed to stop in its motion near Regulus, the King's Star. Over the next few nights it circled Regulus, making a total of three passes around the star.

"Rab-Mag, I know the wandering stars move back and forth across the heavens, but is there any meaning to this?"

"To what, my son?"

"To Jupiter. A few nights ago it stopped its motion

in the constellation of Leo, then circled back around Regulus. It has now passed Regulus three times in the past month or two. Look at my star charts. See the path Jupiter took? Does this mean anything?"

"Did you say Jupiter has been circling Regulus for the past few nights? And you never said anything to me?" Milan asked incredulously. He pondered this for a couple of minutes before continuing, "Arcturus, what were you thinking? Why didn't you tell me? Can it be? Here in my time and I almost missed it! The sign! The sign! The sign!" he said with great excitement. "How many generations of Magi have waited for The Sign, and now God is speaking to us through the stars and giving us His sign. Arcturus, tell me again the behavior of Jupiter."

I didn't understand what Rab-Mag was excited about, after all it was my job to see the whole sky, not just the behavior of one or two stars. And, any observation made on a single night was not enough to make a definite reading of the heavens. It was only on this night that I was able to compare the charts of the past few nights and see the dance that Jupiter was making around Regulus. "Well," I replied, "tonight

I was comparing the position of Jupiter to Regulus, and observing the path it was following. Look here." I unrolled all the star charts from the past few nights and showed him Jupiter's position. "See how it moved back and forth across the sky, then looped around Regulus?"

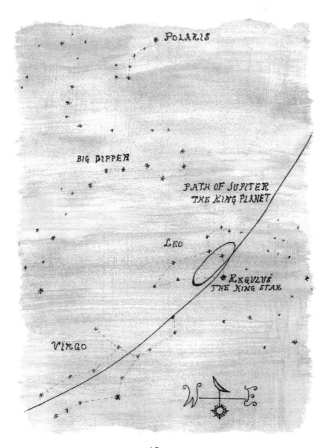

"Yes" he said slowly. "I have seen this before, but maybe it was 20 or more years ago, and it didn't circle Regulus like what you are showing me here. This is significant, but it might not be enough for me to make any conclusions."

"Should we call for the council to meet?" I asked.

"No, I don't think so. But here's what I want you to do. Go to Gaspar's apprentice and discreetly inquire of him what kind of observations of Jupiter he's made. Then come back and report to me," he ordered.

"Yes Rab-Mag. As you wish. I will go right away."

"No, wait. Go tomorrow. Too many questions might be asked if you go now. Tomorrow drop by Gaspar's house on your way to the market, and visit with Shobab."

Shobab was Gaspar's apprentice, and my best friend, too. Gaspar was quite used to me dropping by and spending time with Shobab, so it would have been perfectly natural for me to visit in the afternoon. "Ok, I'll go tomorrow."

The next day I went to see Shobab, as was my habit. We went out into the marketplace, as I had to pick up some supplies for Milan. "So, how goes your observations, Shobab?"

"Oh, you know. Nothing too unusual. Although Gaspar got excited last night when I told him about Jupiter's recent behavior."

Ahh, so Shobab had noticed the wandering star's odd path, too. And Gaspar was excited, too – interesting. "Jupiter's behavior?"

"Yes, of course. You've not seen it? I must be a better apprentice than you!" he joked. "Jupiter has been traveling a most interesting path, seeming to go from east to west, then stop and loop back around Regulus. It has done a full loop around Regulus. Gaspar nearly fainted when I showed him my charts. He kept mumbling something about a coronation, but I didn't know what he was talking about. After all, we already have a king. I pressed him for more answers, but he wouldn't tell me anything more. He actually wanted me to inquire of you, to see what you knew."

"Well, I might have to back and study the charts again. I don't think Rab-Mag would take too kindly if I missed something as important as this. But, I'm sure it's probably nothing. You know how these things are." We continued getting supplies and then went our separate ways.

I ran home as quickly as I could to tell Milan what I had found out. "Rab-Mag! Rab-Mag!" I yelled breathlessly.

"What? What? My son. Tell me. What did you find out?"

"Shobab knows. Gaspar kept saying something about a coronation," I said as I tried to catch my breath. "What does it all mean? You must tell me, Rab-Mag. I know I am only your apprentice, but how can I learn the ways of the Magi unless you tell me?"

"Patience, my son, patience. All will be revealed in good time. I think it is safe to say that if Gaspar thinks what I am thinking, then the others must be thinking it too. Arcturus, I want you to convene a meeting of the council. We must meet quickly. Relay a message to all the Magi that we are to meet tomorrow morning at the third hour. Tell them that they must bring their charts with them. Take my horse and go quickly." "Yes, Rab-Mag, I'll do it right away." So I immediately left to make the announcement.

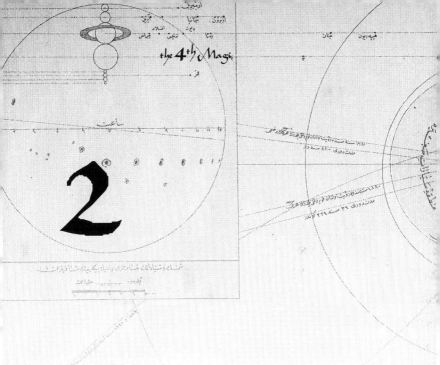

The Magi were a hereditary priesthood descended from the Medes. One did not become a Magi by choice, rather you were born into the priesthood. Since I was adopted into Milan's family, I was accorded the right to be trained in the ways of the Magi. The Magi were renowned as interpreters of dreams, and it was under the reign of Darius the Great that perhaps the most famous Magus of all, Daniel, rose to prominence. The Magi served a dual civil and political role, they made the Council of the Megistanes which had the authority to appoint the king of a realm. Thus, the Magi also had earned the nickname of "King Makers."

This was the first time that the full Council of the Megistanes had met in several months. Often the various Magi were traveling throughout the empire, but it happened that all the Magi were in Persepolis at the same time. For me, this was the place to be because outsiders were not allowed to attend these meetings. Therefore, very few knew of the traditions, rites, ways of the Magi. I felt this to be the utmost privilege to be a part of the council.

All of the Magi were arranged around a large oval table, with Milan occupying the head seat because of his position as Rab-Mag. The table was in the center of a large, marble-floored room that was decorated with paintings of the constellations on the walls and ceiling. Milan's seat was slightly larger than the others; the seat back was ornately carved and inlaid with several jewels befitting his stature.

The other eleven Magi sat in rank order starting on the right and working around the table: Gaspar of Babylon, was tall and slim and had a short but pointy beard; pudgy Melchior of Ur, with his long hair gathered into a blue turban, and his beard twirled and tucked into the same turban; stout Balthasar of Memphis in Egypt, always frowning, but occasionally breaking out with a smile. Larvandad of Sidon, was short and heavy, and always complaining about the pain in his leg. Hormisdas of the Indus Valley was a large man, both in stature and girth and was dressed in his very colorful robes of silk, and wore shoes that curled up at the toe. Gushrasaph of Doris in Asia Minor wore his leather vest over a robe that covered his broad chest, but extended only to his knees. Kagba of Chalcedon in Asia Minor had an outfit similar to Gushrasaph, except that his vest had bronze rivets around the shoulder area. Big and strong Badadilma of Herat had a long shirt that extended to his knees with baggy pants underneath. Bithisarea of Damascus wore a patch over his left eye because of a wound he sustained in his youth; he had on a cotton shirt with puffy sleeves, and a red vest made of silk, along with a skirt-like cloth that came down to his calves. Zimri and Gathaspa were both from Caesarea Philipi and wore simple garments: white robes gathered together with leather belts. We apprentices sat behind the Magi, and there were also representatives from King Phraataces court.

Milan rose and spoke, "Council of the Megistanes, it is good to see all of you here and in good health. We have not met like this in quite some time, and I'm sure that we have a lot to get caught up on. I wish we could devote more time to pleasantries but there is a matter that has come to my attention, which I believe is of the utmost priority, and may require quick and decisive action on our part. Perhaps you already know that of which I am about to speak, or maybe you don't; nevertheless I will explain from the beginning.

"Our forefathers foretold of one who is yet to come who will be the Messiah to all peoples. The Torah is full of passages referring to him: *He will be a prophet like Moses[2]; a descendent of Noah's son Shem[3], and also of Abraham[4], Isaac[5], Jacob[6]; of the house of David[7]; born in Bethlehem[8] of a virgin[9]; a priest after the order of Melchisedek[10]; he will come while the Temple in Jerusalem is still standing[11]; and he will perform many miracles[12]. He will be betrayed by a friend[13]; sold for 30 pieces of silver[14]; he will be spit upon and beaten[15]; and he will be pierced for our transgressions[16]. He will be buried with the rich[17]; though his body will not decay[18]. He will be resurrected from the dead[19]; and will ascend into Heaven[20] where he will be seated at the right hand of God[21]. He will be called the Son of God[22].* All these have been foretold, and are well known by us all.

"Let me also remind you of the prophecy in the Fourth Book of Moses, *'I look into the future, and I see the nation of Israel. A king, like a bright star, will arise in that nation.[23]'* Furthermore, the great Rab-Mag Daniel foretold *'Seven times seventy years is the length of time God has set for freeing your people and your holy city from sin and evil. Sin will be forgiven and eternal justice established, so that the vision and the prophecy will come true, and the holy Temple will be rededicated.[24]'* You have been looking for the fulfillment of this prophecy as earnestly as I, and are well acquainted with the fact that the calculation of those years brings us to this period of time.

"My brothers, I believe that the time has come for these prophecies to be fulfilled. Two nights ago my young apprentice Arcturus was reviewing his celestial charts, and brought to my attention that the wandering star Jupiter has been behaving in a manner that caused me to convene this council. I sent Arcturus out to inquire of Shobab, Gaspar's apprentice, to see if he had made the same observations (I know it was a little sneaky and underhanded, but I had to keep up the appearance of normalcy), and he came back to me quite excitedly to confirm our observations. So let me take time to applaud Arcturus and Shobab for their good work." Shobab was glaring at me first, because of what Milan had just said, but with all the applause for him and I it did not take long for him to burst out with a broad grin. But both of our smiles quickly turned sour when Milan declared "And now I would like to ask our two fine apprentices to share their discoveries with all of us now." Several dozen eyes turned their gaze in our direction.

I immediately felt my face and ears turn hot and broke out in a sweat as I realized that I had just been called upon to speak to the Council of the Megistanes. I began to shake in my sandals, and my throat suddenly felt very dry. I looked over at Shobab, and saw that what I was suffering from was contagious.

I cleared my throat, stood up and began to speak "Uh, hello, my name is Arcturus. I am an apprentice under Milan, and was raised in the School of the Magi in Persepolis. I feel quite unworthy to speak to you this morning, as I still have much to learn. I maintain the celestial charts for my master as part of my duties. The other night I noticed that Jupiter had been following a path from east to west, but then stopped in its path and reversed its course. This happened in the constellation of Leo. Jupiter then appeared to circle around Regulus, or Regulus. Of course, this didn't become apparent until I had charts from several nights to compare with each other. I asked my master Milan if this was of any significance, and he immediately got excited. I don't have much more to add than that." Then I sat down.

Everyone's attention then turned to Shobab. "I, um, don't have much to add, either," Shobab said nervously. "I, too, noticed Jupiter's odd path as Arcturus did. I didn't know what to make of it, though, so I asked Gaspar if there was anything to it. I must say that I was pretty surprised by Gaspar's reaction. I thought he was going to faint, because his face turned pale, his knees almost buckled, and he hoarsely whispered 'It's time! It's time! Praise God, it's time.'"

Milan smiled with approval, then said "Gentlemen, this is just one sign, but it is significant nonetheless.

We have the King's Star being crowned by the King's Wandering Star."

Gaspar piped up, "A coronation."

"Yes, a coronation," Milan said in agreement. "I believe that a new king will soon be here."

The other Magi sat there expressionless for a few seconds as the weight of Milan's words sank in. Was this heavenly event truly a sign of new kingship? If so, did it signify the arrival of the Messiah? Gushrasaph cleared his throat and then said, "Men and brothers, I have listened intently to the words of the Rab-Mag and find his reasoning compelling, however I must ask that we not jump to conclusions. I agree that the behavior of Jupiter is most interesting, but I am not immediately led to believe that this signifies anything regarding the Messiah. I see how Gaspar arrives at the conclusion of a coronation, but a coronation of whom? What king and what kingdom? Keep in mind that we are known throughout the land as king makers, and it would be quite an embarrassment to us if we are wrong on this. I would argue that we need to exercise more caution, and perhaps continue to watch the heavens to see what else they might tell us."

Larvandad nodded in agreement, "Yes, I think that it would be wise for all of us to consider what Milan has said, but to also take more time to read the stars. We know that the wandering stars are in the habit of moving according to their own will. We have seen how they are able to move in one direction, then stop and move in another. Milan talks about the Messiah, and perhaps he is right. This much I do know: Jupiter has passed by Regulus three times, and has actually followed a path encircling the King's Star. To me this says 'King! King! King!' It is interesting that this is taking place in the sign of Leo, but do we leap to the conclusion that this signifies The Lion of Judah, the Messiah promised generations ago? I am hesitant to say yes."

Gathaspa, the most junior of the Magi then spoke, "Men and brothers, I have heard words for and against acting on the sign of Jupiter, and both sides have been persuasive. But as I have studied the prophecies and seen the signs in the heavens, I am led to believe that Milan is right. Furthermore, Milan is the Rab-Mag, and did not ascend to this position by blind luck. Also, I have spent many years apprenticing under him, just as Arcturus is doing now, and know that he would not recklessly convene the Council of the Magistenes unless he had a convincing reason. I think that these particular signs speak of a king, and if I were to gamble I would say that they refer to the promised Messiah, because of the timing of the sign coinciding with Rab-Mag Daniel's prophecy. The prophet Micah tells that he will be born in Bethlehem[25]. But here's what we don't know: has the Messiah already come or is he yet to come?"

Gathaspa's comments hung heavy in the air. The possibility that the Messiah had already come and that the Magi had missed the event seemed worrisome. The Promised One was to be the ruler of nations, not just the leader of some far-flung insignificant district. Surely someone of this stature needed the Magi to confirm his kingship. It was clear by the expressions on the Magi's faces that a decision needed to be made. Should the Magi stay in Parthia, or should they journey to Judea?

Milan finally broke the silence. "My brothers, I understand the hesitation some of you may have about this matter, but I believe that we are compelled to act. I believe that this council must coronate the new king, and I believe that time is of the essence. As you know, it is a long journey, and it will take many months to get to Jerusalem. Therefore, I propose we leave Persepolis right away for Siraf and board a ship bound for the Red Sea. This would allow us to make good time without stopping every night like we would if we traveled by land. We will disembark from there and join a caravan bound for Jerusalem, and from there inquire about the location of the new king. I suspect that he would be somewhere in the royal palace, likely in the inner chambers of the king's court, so we will need to bear gifts. Does anyone know the name of the King of Jerusalem?"

"The Romans have installed a man named Herod," reported Zimri, who had returned from a lengthy trip to the region about six months ago. "He rules Judea with an iron fist. He has an uneasy alliance with the Jewish priesthood, notably a sect called the Pharisees. Herod is a shrewd man. He is quick to quash anything he perceives to be a threat. I do not know how he will react to the news of the Messiah's arrival. Perhaps he is a religious man, and would welcome the news. On the other hand, he might just make out the Messiah to be a threat to his throne and would do anything to kill him. No doubt the Jewish priesthood has counted the years since Rab-Mag Daniel's prophecy and are in equal anticipation of his arrival as we are. This probably means that Herod is aware of the prophecies, too, but that is just a guess on my part. I would think that we would not be able to speak directly to the Jewish authorities without going through Herod, so caution would be the virtue of the day in dealing with him. One other thing," he added, "This journey is fraught with many dangers and perils. If we travel by land, there will be bandits along the way. And if we travel by sea, there will be pirates. Vigilance is of the utmost importance."

"Thank you Zimri for your report. This information will no doubt prove useful when we meet him face to face. I believe that the time has come for us to decide on the path we should take. We will take a secret vote. Each Magus will make his mark on a parchment and place his vote in the clay jar. Arcturus will count the votes once they are all in." instructed Milan.

The Magi took their time pondering what to do. This was not a decision to be made lightly. The outcome of the vote would dictate whether the Magi would journey westward to Judea to crown the new king. I imagined the Messiah to be a young man, probably eighteen years old or so, ready to take the throne. Perhaps Herod had already yielded to him, and the Messiah was consolidating his power. The icy grip of Rome could be felt even here in Parthia; surely this Messiah was organizing forces to vanquish the despised Latins and their pantheon of gods. If it were up to me, we would mount up on our camels and begin the journey immediately.

After what seemed to be an hour or so the final vote was cast. Milan nodded at me to take the jar and count the ballots. I signaled for Shobab to come to my side as I counted. He ran over and sat next to me; he reached into the jar and handed me the first ballot…

It took me about a minute to count all the votes. "Arcturus, what is the result?" inquired Milan. "Rab-Mag, seven Magi have voted to make the journey, and five have voted not to."

So it was decided. The Magi would assemble within a week to begin the journey. Of the five who voted against going, three decided in the end to make the trip, while two remained resolute in staying behind. Thus, there would ten Magi making the trip: Milan, Gaspar, Melchior, Balthasar, Gushrasaph, Kagba, Badadilma, Bithisarea, Zimri and Gathaspa. Hormisdas and Larvandad would remain in Parthia.

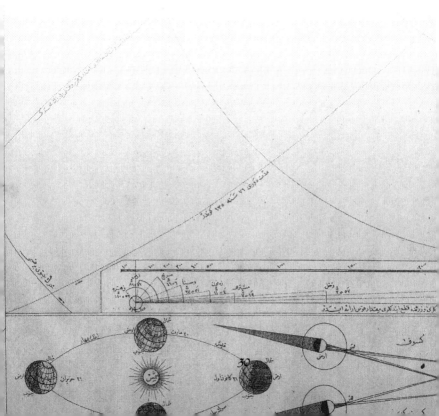

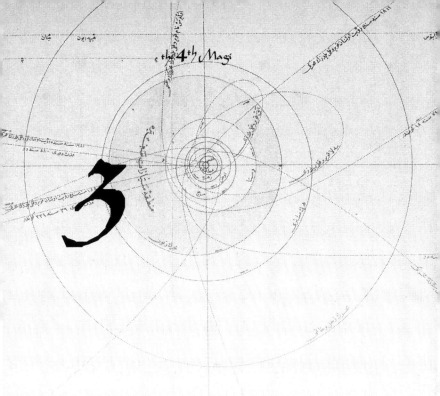

The Magi assembled together in the marketplace. All of the apprentices, along with other hired hands, had been working hard getting provisions together for the journey that lay ahead. In all, there would be about forty of us making the trip. The easiest part of the trip would be the first leg to the port city of Siraf, Milan's home town. From there we would board a sea-going vessel, rounding the Arabian Peninsula to the Red Sea. We planned to disembark at the ancient port of Muza in Arabia, and then caravan along the Red Sea coastline to the Gulf of Aqabah, then cross over the River Jordan and head west from there to Jerusalem. Milan estimated the journey to take three or four months, depending on the availability of ships to take us, and then waiting on a caravan for us to join for the overland portion along the Red Sea coast.

Milan made his way down to the docks at Siraf. This was a place known for its collection of scoundrels, dens of thieves, liars, and otherwise miserable characters. Milan said that Siraf was no different than any other port city; sailors were sailors no matter where you went, and the one thing you could count on was for your pocket to be picked before you even knew a pickpocket was about.

Milan came to the first ship and strode aboard. "I wish to speak to the captain," he announced to the deckhand.

"The captain is busy and doesn't want to be disturbed," came the quick reply.

"I see. Well, if he is too busy, perhaps I can take my business elsewhere. When you get a chance, tell him that he just missed an opportunity to make 30 gold pieces. Thank you for your time. Good day."

And with that, Milan turned his back to head back down to the dock.

"Thirty gold pieces!?! Just a minute, fine sir. Let me see if the captain is finished with his business. I'll be right back." And with that the deckhand was off. He returned a few minutes later with a most unruly-looking, foul-smelling fellow. It looked as if he had just woken up from being drunk for the past few nights.

"I am Captain Cornelius," he slurred. "What can I do for you?"

"Well, Captain Cornelius, I need a vessel to take me and my companions from here to Muza. Can you accommodate us?"

"And how many are there in your party?"

"Forty total, along with provisions and luggage."

"Forty! Thirty pieces of gold will not be enough for that many. I will not take less than eighty." Even in a drunken stupor the captain still had enough business sense to negotiate a deal.

"I am afraid your price is too high. I cannot give you more than thirty five."

"My good man, I have to maintain my ship and pay my crew a decent wage. Thirty five won't even be enough to unfurl the sails. How about seventy."

"I'll tell you what. I will give you forty five now and ten more upon completion of the journey. I believe that is a fair offer. It is also my final offer."

"Sir, you have yourself a ship."

"Very good. How soon before you will be ready to set sail?"

"We can be ready in three days."

"Three days it is. Our party will be here. We expect to make good speed, Captain Cornelius. I cannot reveal the purpose of our journey, except to say that we must reach Muza within two weeks."

"Muza in two weeks! We will have to have favorable winds the whole way, and only make one, maybe two port calls along the way. It can be done, but it won't be easy. You must also know that we are nearing typhoon season. At any time a tempest can rise up that could swallow a ship whole."

"I understand the risks, and I am undeterred."

"Very well."

"Very well. And good day to you."

And with that the transaction was completed.

We returned to Persepolis to tell the others of the

arrangements we made. While the Magi were used to traveling, never before had the so many made such a journey together.

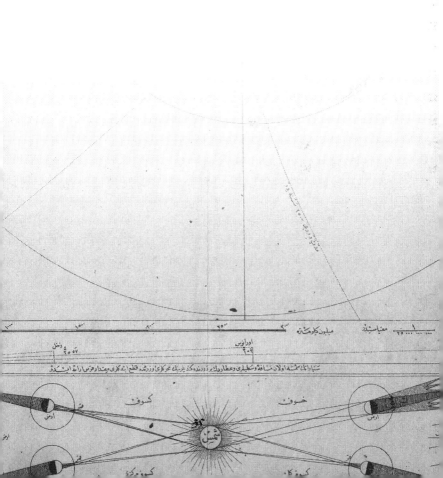

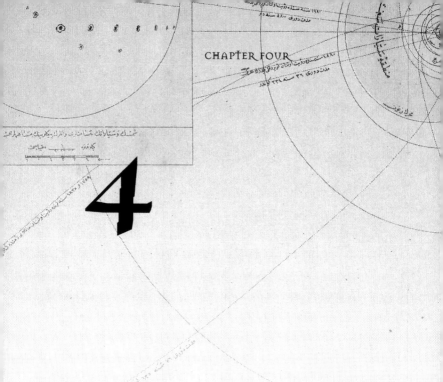

4

The entire entourage arrived in Siraf on the third day. To me it seemed as if our expedition couldn't begin soon enough. We made our way down to the docks and boarded the vessel that would take us on the first leg. We were led down below to where our quarters would be for the voyage. Our belongings were stored in the hold in the bottom deck.

It became quickly apparent that we were out of place among these sailors. They were a ragtag bunch of unruly, smelly, dirty, crude people, whose only joy was to make our journey as miserable as possible. The

Magi were accustomed to spending time among the educated and the elite of Parthia and other nations. It seemed to us that though we were on the same boat as they, in reality we were worlds apart from these seafarers. My hope was that we would make it to our destination without having our throats slit and our bodies tossed overboard in the middle of the night. And yet, Rab-Mag didn't seem to be put off in the least by the sailors. In the evening he would sit up on the deck and regale them with stories of his travels and adventures. In doing so, he managed to develop a sort of affection for them, not seeing them as the dregs of society, but as ordinary people whose lot in life was to live on the sea.

Our journey began rather slowly, as the winds weren't favorable on the Parthian Gulf. It took us about four days to make it to the Arabian Sea where we picked up the Trade Winds that took us along the coast of Arabia. You would think that we would be used to the rocking motion of the ship, having traveled most of our lives on camels, but it did not take long for us to begin "feeding the fish," suffering from sea-sickness that didn't seem to end. Of course, the sailors rollicked in laughter every time one of our party was bent over the rail retching violently.

It was about the tenth day of our journey that Captain Cornelius ordered us to lash everything securely because there was a storm brewing. I looked around in every direction, but didn't see so much as a puff of cloud. I wondered if he was attempting to trick us so that we would be the butt of another joke for the sailors, but there was something in his voice that even the sailors reacted to. Captain Cornelius had been a sailor all his life, and the sailors placed their trust in his skill and ability to take them safely to each port. Obviously, he knew how to read the subtleties of the winds far better than anyone else on board, so when warned of the coming storm the sailors heeded his instructions and immediately set about to prepare for it.

Sure enough, about three hours later dark clouds began to form in the east. A short time after, a stiff wind began to blow, and the waves reached a height of about six feet. A few hours later the storm was upon us, and the waves were now twenty to thirty feet. The rain came down as if we were in a waterfall, and there was no place that we could hide in the ship that would keep us from getting wet. We were thrown up and down, left and right, forward and backward, with no relief in sight. Even the most seasoned of the sailors cried out in fear.

It seemed as if the storm would never end. The captain and some of the crew battled the storm on the main deck, but we were a most wretched lot, cowering in fear below deck. We could hear the captain bellow orders, but it seemed to us that his efforts were to no avail.

Then, without warning things turned very bad. We heard an ear-splitting crash of thunder, and a few seconds later the mast snapped and crashed through the deck on top of several of us. There were yells and screams from above and below us. Water was flooding through the gaping hole every time a wave washed over the deck. Every flash of lightning showed a dismal picture. The wind caused the broken mast to smash left and right, causing more destruction with each move. And the screams continued. The storm did not let up. We cried out to God to save us, but it seemed that the wind was drowning out our pleas and

He couldn't hear us.

Then, when we thought things could get no worse, a lookout yelled out, "ROCKS! ROCKS AHEAD! WE'RE ABOUT TO CRASH!"

The captain tried to steer away, but the force of the storm was too overwhelming, and his feeble efforts did nothing to slow the inevitable.

Suddenly the ship shuddered violently. There was a terrible creaking and groaning from throughout the ship. Suddenly water was coming up from below as well as coming down from above. We were all doomed. It did not take but a few minutes for the ship to be torn to pieces.

I was hurled into the water and immediately panicked. None of our party knew how to swim. I frantically tried to keep my head above water, but the weight of my clothes kept pulling me down. My head slipped below the surface, and I swallowed an enormous amount of water and began to drown. But, in my frantic thrashing about I caught hold of a piece of wood. I held onto it with all my might as I bobbed to the surface.

I gasped and coughed and threw up everything

that was in me. I was alive, but barely. Then, without warning, I was thrown up onto the shore. I lay there motionless, thoroughly exhausted and spent.

I think I lay there for hours, but I really don't know how much time had passed. The sun was up and the wind had died down to almost nothing now. Every muscle in my body ached. I was bruised, and scraped up pretty badly, but nothing more serious than that. I picked up my head and looked around. All around me was debris from the shipwreck. I could hear moans and groans from various places along the shore, but I did not see anyone.

I tried to stand up to walk, but my legs were wobbly beneath me. There was a stick two or three feet away from me that looked like it could be used for a walking stick, so I crawled over to it, then used it to pull myself up. Every step I took was tortuous, but at least I was able to walk. I went about thirty yards or so and came upon the first body. It was Zimri. It looked as if he had been impaled in his back by a plank. Not far from him lay Kagba, with the body of one of the sailors draped over his back. Both were motionless. A few yards further down the beach sat

Melchior with what appeared to be a broken arm and maybe some bruises. I made my way over to him and sat next to him. "Melchior, are you okay?" He looked at me with a very far away look. Finally he focused on me. "Arcturus," he said hoarsely.

"My lord, not everyone survived. Zimri and Kagba are dead. I haven't found anyone else yet. What should we do?"

Melchior was slow to respond. Finally he replied, "We must tend to the survivors. Help me up."

It took some effort to get him up, but he stood fully erect once he was up. He seemed to be coming to his senses now. "Let's walk down the shore this way and see what we can find."

The debris was scattered over roughly a mile in total. We came across several bodies, but they all seemed to be of the ship's crew. We turned around and headed in the other direction, past the point where Zimri and Kagba lay. The next Magus we came across was Badadilma. He was alive, but seemed to be in pretty bad shape. He had a nasty gash across his forehead, and his left leg lay in an awkward position. I didn't know how to tend to him, aside from somehow trying to bring comfort to him. Melchior immediately wrapped a cloth around the wound on his head, but when he tried to set his leg Badadilma cried out in pain.

"His leg is broken. We must find some planks that we can use as splints to keep his leg from moving. It should be pretty easy to find them with all the wreckage about. Bring as much as you can, as I am certain we will come across more survivors whose wounds will need to be tended to."

In a few minutes I had collected a pretty good pile of planks. We found two that were of appropriate length to splint Badadilma's leg. He protested in every way, but we finally managed to set the splint.

Melchior and I continued to look for other survivors. It did not take long. Captain Cornelius was kneeling next to another sailor, tending to his wounds. Another sailor seemed to be busy working on fashioning a crude sun shelter with some wood and tattered sails. Just beyond them we found the rest of the Magi: Milan, Gaspar, Balthasar, Gushrasaph, Bithisarea, and Gathaspa. Milan had a broken rib and several cuts, but nothing more. Gaspar had some severe bruises, but it didn't look like anything was broken. Balthasar had a broken nose, but Melchior reset it much to his objections. Gushrasaph, Bithisarea, and Gathaspa all appeared to be okay for the most part, aside from maybe some cuts and scrapes. All told, there were twenty-two survivors.

Of course, I immediately tended to Milan. I was overjoyed to see that he had made it through the disaster with only a broken rib. "Oh Master, I was worried for you!"

"My son, I am relieved to see you alive and walking around. Are you hurt?"

"I am fine. Just a little stiff. I will be okay. Have you seen Shobab?"

"No. I don't think any of us have seen him."

"Master, he's my best friend. I must go and find him."

"Yes, my son, go and search for him. We are not going anywhere, soon."

I continued further down the beach, until I came to last of the debris from our shipwreck. I saw a few more bodies, all crewmen, but could not find my dear friend. He and I practically grew up together since the age of two. We had been inseparable for so long that many thought we were brothers. And in many ways, we were brothers. I struggled to fight back tears as I searched for him. I could not bear the thought of losing him to this terrible storm. I turned around and headed back toward where the others were. There was a large piece of wreckage from the bow that had come ashore, but the bulk of it was partially submerged with waves battering the ragged opening of the ship. Perhaps Shobab was still in there.

It took a lot of painful effort to climb into the wreck, but I eventually made it to the top. It was very difficult to stand up because the wreck was tilted sharply to one side, and then was heaving up and down with each wave that broke against the opening. I called out, "Shobab! Shobab! Where are you?"

I paused to listen, but could only hear the sound of the surf. I cautiously made my way to the hatch that led to the decks below and awkwardly poked my head down and called out again. And again, I heard nothing. But then, it seemed that a low moan was coming from somewhere inside. I didn't know if it was the sound of the wreck groaning in the surf, or if perhaps there was someone still trapped below. No matter, I had to find out. Shobab could still be down there.

There was a tangled rope lying off to one side. I tied one end to the rail, and then made a loop around my chest with the other end. I then crept back over to the lip of the opening, looked in, and then dropped down below. Over in one corner lay a pile of debris over six feet high. Laying face down on top of the heap was someone, obviously hurt, but quite alive. I climbed up to him, picked up his head, and felt his breath on my cheek. It was Shobab.

I didn't know how to get him down from where he was, and I didn't know exactly how badly hurt he was. The only thing I could think of was to go back out and get some help. I climbed back up to the upper deck using the rope, then scrambled off the wreck and down to the beach. Then as quickly as I could manage, I went back to the others. "I found Shobab. He's on the wreck and he's badly hurt. I don't know how to get him down from where he is. I need help!"

Gushrasaph, Bithisarea, and Gathaspa, the three Magi who had made out the best, immediately got to their feet and followed me to the wreck. Gathaspa took charge and ordered me to stay on the beach while he and Bithisarea climbed up onto the wreck. It took about twenty minutes for them to get Shobab off and down to the shore. He was in a lot of pain, and looked quite battered. We used some torn sail and two poles off the wreck to make a litter to carry him back to others. I was in fear for my best friend's life.

Milan had had formal training as a physician, part of his royal duties before King Phraateces, and was tending to the wounded as best as he was able. When we arrived with Shobab, he immediately devoted his attention to my friend. "We must find some fresh water for him. Not just for him, but for all of us. It will be midday soon, and the heat will get quite unbearable. Captain, what sort of fresh water stores do you have on board your ship?"

Captain Cornelius paused at the question. "We have barrels of water stowed on both decks, but I'm afraid that most of them would have either washed away or broken open. We must organize a party to retrieve whatever freshwater barrels we can find." He called for his crewmen to begin looking for whatever provisions they could recover. It took a couple of hours for them to scour the beach for anything useable; in the end they were able to find a couple of intact barrels of freshwater, some dry food, and a barrel of salted fish. Not much, but it would sustain us for a couple of days.

Meanwhile, Milan had some hard decisions to make. Clearly, not everyone in our party could continue on from here. It was possible that if we waited a month or two, a couple more of our party would have recovered to the point that they could carry on. Unfortunately, Captain Cornelius didn't know quite where we were along the Arabian coast; none of our charts or other navigation devices survived the shipwreck. Therefore, we didn't know how close we were to any settlements and possible help. It turned out we didn't have to wait very long.

As the sun was getting lower in the sky, one of the sailors sitting on a grassy dune cried out, "Caravan, ho!" Those of us who could walk immediately jumped up and ran over to where he was. Sure enough, approaching us from the east was a caravan of about three dozen camels. A few minutes later they were upon us.

Milan acted as the spokesman for all of us. "Peace be with you," he greeted, "We are glad you are here. We were shipwrecked in last night's storm. We have wounded among us, some of whom are in pretty bad shape. Are you able to help us?"

The travelers immediately dismounted their camels. They each had long, curved swords sheathed around their chests, along with a couple of daggers tucked into their waist belts. They looked like a pretty tough lot, and we didn't know if they meant us harm or not. The biggest of them came to the front. "Peace be with you. I am Simeon, leader of this caravan. We are journeying to Arabia. We are glad to help you." We all breathed a little easier with relief. "We have some medicine, but not enough for all your wounded. There is a village about half-a-day's journey from here, perhaps there is a doctor there. I will leave some of my men here to help you; go ahead and put your wounded on our camels."

Milan nodded in agreement. We immediately placed the most severely hurt on the camels. Most of the wounded were sailors, but Badadilma and Shobab would also need tending at the village. Unfortunately, they would not be able to make the journey to Jerusalem with us.

"Where was your intended destination?" asked Simeon.

"Jerusalem. We are Magi from Parthia. We saw signs in the heavens that we believe are revealing the arrival of the Messiah."

"The Messiah!" exclaimed Simeon. "Many generations have long awaited his arrival. You believe he has come?"

"Yes, the signs are all there," replied Milan. "We boarded this ship in Parthia because we reasoned that sailing would get us there quicker than going by caravan. Now we are shipwrecked, the storm claimed two of our own, and two more are too wounded to go on. Thankfully, your caravan will take our wounded to be tended to, but we will be unable to get to Jerusalem."

"You need not worry, Milan. We too are Jews. We are spice traders. We travel throughout the region selling the finest spices, perfumes, and oils. This area is well known for its myrrh, and we are well known for the quality of myrrh we produce. We also trade in cinnamon, cardamom, cloves, saffron, sumac, thyme, sesame seeds, and many others. We will take you to where you need to go. If indeed the Messiah has come, then we do not want to miss him either. We aren't as fast as a ship, but if this is of God, then timing is not a worry. I have learned that His timing is always perfect."

Tears welled up in Milan's eyes. He had just lost two very good friends in Zimri and Kagba. He also was disappointed that Badadilma wouldn't be able to make the rest of the journey. And of course, he was very concerned about Shobab's condition. But he also was reassured that the journey to Jerusalem would continue. "Praise be to God," Milan responded. "Your kindness and generosity are too much to repay."

"Think nothing of it. It is for the Messiah."

"Yes. For the Messiah."

It was later the following day that the caravan returned from taking the wounded to the nearest village. The rest of us who were able-bodied gathered anything of value from the debris of the wreck to take with us. We were able to recover much of our personal belongings, for they had been stored toward the bow of the ship. The sailors, however, didn't fare so well, as most of their belongings were lost. The Magi and the traders shared from their wealth to ensure that they would be able to replenish that which was lost.

All of us traveled to the village where Badadilma and Shobab were. We were relieved to see that they were being well taken care of. Badadilma's leg was swollen and black and blue, but it looked like he would recover in due time. My dear friend Shobab was a different story. He was lying in a bed with his head propped up. His face was puffed out, with his eyes almost swollen shut. His right hand was curled in toward his body in an awkward fashion, and his left leg was clearly broken, although the town physician had set it with some sticks for a splint. It was clear that his recovery would take much longer.

Shobab opened one eye as much as he could to look at me. "Arcturus, my brother. I must be quite a sight to see," he rasped. "It looks like you fared better than I. Thanks for coming to find me."

"I had to find you, Shobab. There's no way I could have done anything else but look for you. You are like my own flesh and blood. We have been through so much together. We now have quite a story to tell our children, though."

Shobab chuckled at that thought, although his smile was quickly replaced with a grimace from pain. "You know I can't go on with you, don't you," he said matter-of-factly. "I would have liked to have seen the Messiah. Please tell him about me."

"I can't go on without you, Shobab. We are in a strange place among strange people. You need me to take care of you."

"Nonsense. I am sure Badadilma will make sure that I am well taken care of. You are on a mission to see the Messiah. My brother, you must go on. You must fulfill what God has in store for you. I will be very angry with you if you don't go."

I tried to hold back the tears, but was unsuccessful. I also knew that what he was saying was true. I wanted to embrace him, but I didn't know where I could touch him that wouldn't hurt him, so I held his left hand, something that was not customary for our people to do. "I will tell the Messiah all about you," I said tearfully. "I will tell him how you longed to see him. I will make sure that he knows who you are. Farewell Shobab. I will come back for you."

"Farewell Arcturus. May God go with you."

With that I turned and walked out of the room. I wept like I had never wept before. There never was a time in my life that I was apart from Shobab. And now I was going to make the journey of a lifetime without him.

With that, we mounted up and began the next leg of our trek.

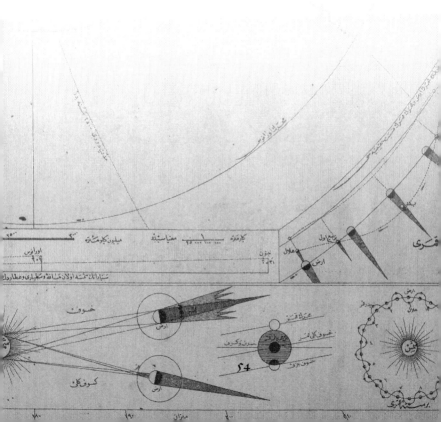

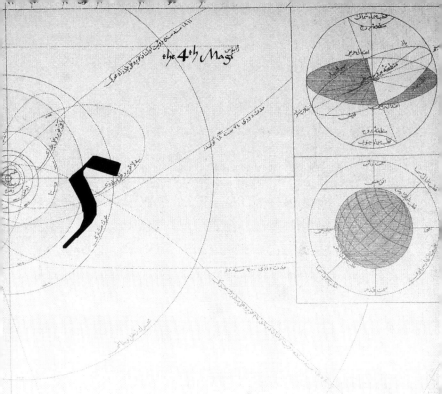

the 4th Magi

Our next destination was the ancient city of Sheba. This is the city where the famed Queen of Sheba was from, the royal visitor to King Solomon so many centuries ago. It would take us about 2 or 3 days to make the trek. The plan was for us to rest for a day or two while gathering enough provisions for the next leg. There was a possibility of us joining with another larger caravan that was preparing to leave; the advantage would be greater protection from thieves and bandits, but the disadvantage was that it might slow us down. Simeon and Milan were going to make that decision for us. In the meantime I had the opportunity to explore a new city.

I went down to the marketplace to see what I could find. Things here seemed to be much more chaotic than what I was used to in Parthia. Traders were coming and going with their goods from distant lands. The merchants all spoke in a tongue I was unfamiliar with, but it seemed that their language was close enough to mine that I could make out many of the words. The air was filled with the aroma of many different spices, some I had never smelled before. The colorful spices were piled high on large, round, metal dishes.

"Young man," a chicken merchant beckoned, "Take your pick of the finest chickens in town."

Another summoned, "Come here. Come and see my fine silk. It came all the way from India."

Others were holding up jewelry, shoes, coats, fruit, and just about everything else that could be sold. I kept walking through the market, looking at all the wares, but finally stopped at one merchant who didn't call for me, but she tempted me with an aroma I hadn't smelled before. "I have the finest frankincense in all of Arabia. My family has been producing it for over a century."

"Frankincense, eh? I have never smelled it before. What is it used for?" I asked.

"It has many different uses. Some varieties have healing powers, others awaken your senses, and others make your skin soft and supple. It is extremely valuable, as costly as gold in many parts of the world." She then opened a small vial and held it up to me. "Breathe this in deeply."

I slowly inhaled a scent that was sweet, almost fruity, with a hint of lemon and pine. I felt a warmth come over me that I had never felt before. "Wow. This is very pleasant."

"Do you have someone special to give it to?" she asked.

"Well, no. I can't think of anyone. I actually don't know anyone here. You see, I am from Parthia, and am just passing through here. I am afraid I would have no use for it. And besides, I don't have much money with me."

"Perhaps there is someone special at your destination? Where are traveling to?"

"I am journeying with several Magi to Jerusalem. We believe that the signs in the heavens declare the

Messiah has come. We are going to see him."

"The Messiah?!? The Magi are traveling to see the Messiah? The Magi are well known, even here in Arabia. Their reputation as king-makers has been known for generations."

"Yes, I am an apprentice magus. We were traveling by ship, but were shipwrecked a few days ago. Two of our number died, and two others are too badly hurt to carry on. We are now preparing to leave by caravan to Jerusalem. As I said, I wouldn't have much use for frankincense. I don't think the Messiah would care for any, either."

"But you must take some!" she cried. "My family has been waiting for the Messiah to come for generations. If the Magi believe he has come, then I believe it to. You must take some, you must. Take it as a gift from my family. Please, I have nothing else to offer him."

"But lady, you said this was more valuable than gold. I cannot just take it from you."

"It is not your place to tell me what I can give and what I cannot!" she said, as if offended. "Yes, what I give you is more valuable than gold. But my family will produce more. What other family will be able to say that their frankincense was used by the Messiah?"

With that she thrust a small jar of her most valuable frankincense into my hands. It probably was worth one or two months wages to her, but I did not have it in my heart to refuse her.

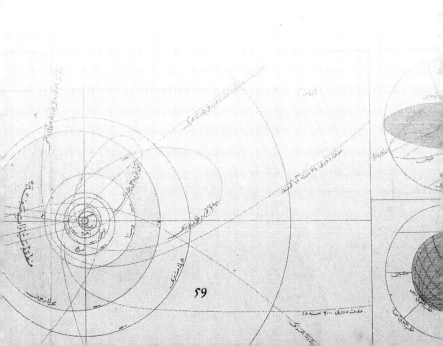

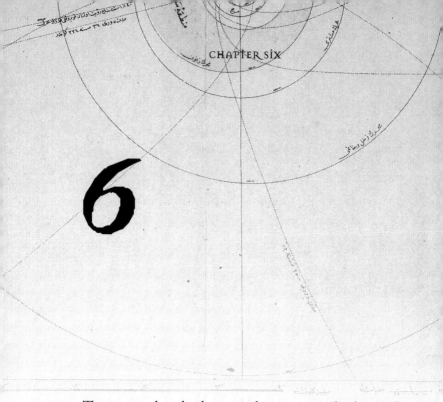

6

Ten months had passed since I had made the observations about Jupiter's celestial path. Unfortunately, my charts had been ruined by the storm and the resulting shipwreck, and I wasn't able to refer back to them. So, I had to start anew; methodically and painstakingly plotting the stars. However, I knew all the constellations and their relative positions to each other by memory, so recreating the night sky wasn't that difficult. The challenge was trying to follow the path of the wandering stars.

None of us expected to see the spectacle we saw

during the day. It was on the seventeenth day of the sixth month that a new star appeared, and it shone with incredible brightness even during the day. In fact, it could clearly be seen high in the sky at noon. All the Magi gathered to see this thing that had no explanation.

As day faded into night it the new star blazed even brighter. The Magi we are all puzzled at this. The Magi became very excited, and all were talking at once. "What sign is this?" Gushrasaph shouted. "Again, this is in the sign of Leo!"

Bithisarea stroked his beard as he looked upward, "But where are Jupiter and Anaitis?"

No one had their ancient chart to refer to, but the Magi didn't need them. Never had this event been observed before, and the Magi had kept meticulous records for hundreds of years. Anaitis, or what the Romans called Venus, had been very close to Jupiter in recent nights. Both were full and bright.

Then it struck him, "Can it be that their light is as one? Have they merged together into one star[26]?"

"This is of utmost importance," Milan emphatically declared. "In all my years I have never observed anything like this. Clearly God is reaffirming the sign of the Messiah to us. Jupiter is the King's Wandering Star. Anaitis is the Mother's Wandering Star. They meet in the sign of Leo. If I put this all together, I would say this signifies the Promised One of the Lion of Judah"

Balthasar piped in, "I say this means that the Messiah is yet to be born! We are not too late, at least not yet!"

Gaspar wasn't so optimistic, "Or, maybe he was born tonight. Or maybe a king is getting married. Or maybe the Messiah is really a queen. Or how about this: a lion is going to eat the king's mother. I wouldn't be so quick to jump to conclusions. Remember, we all came on this venture because of Milan's impassioned argument about the Messiah, but after the shipwreck I can't be so sure."

Milan responded, "Gaspar, you are a Magus with decades of experience. You know as well as I that this sign is unlike any we have seen before. You tell me what you believe this star to be."

Gaspar looked around at the others in the dimness of the night, took a deep breath, then replied, "Milan, I do not dispute that what we have seen tonight is truly remarkable. Nor I dispute your position as Rab-Mag. But, I can't help but wonder if your conclusions are correct. Is it possible that there are other interpretations? Could we be pursuing a fool's chase?

Melchior piped in, "Gaspar, we are all knowledgeable about celestial events. We know stars better than anyone. It is our life's work to know such things. None of us have any other plausible explanation for what we just saw. We have never seen a star suddenly appear overnight. Nor have we ever seen one shine with such radiance that it could be seen at noon. Even if there is another explanation, do we simply turn around and go home? I believe we have come too far to turn around, even if we are wrong. But, if we are right, then it falls upon our shoulders to validate and anoint the Messiah."

Balthasar echoed, "Yes. It falls upon our shoulders to anoint the Messiah."

A chorus of "Amen" rose from the others, to include Simeon and the other caravan drivers.

Gaspar still wasn't convinced, but he conceded, "Brothers, I will continue forward, but only because we have come this far. I would hate for Zimri's and Kagba's death to have been in vain."

With that it was agreed that our expedition would continue on to Jerusalem.

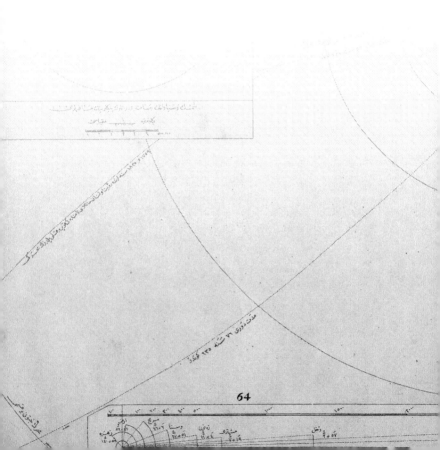

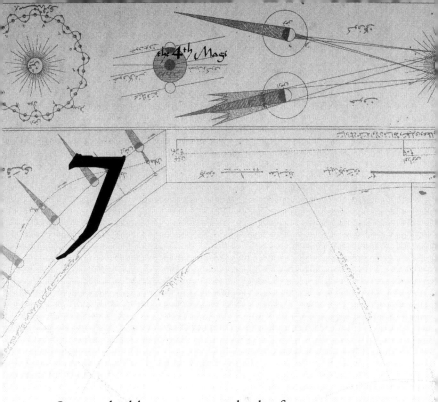

7

Simeon had been a caravan leader for over twenty years. He had traveled throughout the Levant, from Parthia to Babylon, from Sheba to Tyre, and even across North Africa into the Sahara. He had many tales to tell, although there were times when we weren't sure how true they were. He would speak of being caught in sandstorms and whirlwinds, of fights with bandits, of strange and wondrous animals, and of exotic people with beautiful women.

Many times caravans would join together, especially when traveling long distances. This was because there was greater protection in numbers. Many of the routes were notorious for being ambushed by bandits. It was not uncommon for a caravan to lose a third of its camels and cargo to these thieves, thus the camel drivers were skilled with swords and daggers. Even still, bandits always had one advantage: the element of surprise. No matter how well armed the caravaners were, they could only react to an ambush after it started. The ambushes almost always took place in narrow canyons, where the caravan was forced to travel in a line one behind the other, rather than abreast of each other. This made it very difficult for caravaners to come to each other's aid unless they dismounted from their camels, making the camels and their precious cargo vulnerable to thieves who would climb down from their hiding places behind the rocks.

The other advantage the bandits had was that they used horses instead of camels. A horse didn't have the range of a camel in the desert environment, but a bandit need to worry about that because he wouldn't necessarily be traveling any great distance. Speed was the bandit's best friend, and a horse allowed him to swoop down on an unsuspecting caravan.

It was a useless venture to try to chase after the bandits because oftentimes they had the support of the local village (they were probably friends and family of the bandits and accumulated their wealth via stolen loot). One of the tactics a band of bandits would use was to lure young and brash caravaners away from the main body by attacking only with four or five at a time. The caravaner would be duped into thinking that he could chase after these rogues only to find a much larger party laying in wait around a corner or on the other side of a hill. Seasoned caravaners simply counted on bandits as being part of the cost of business. Still, they preferred not to take any unnecessary chances.

Simeon made sure that there were provisions enough for the leg that lay ahead. Although there were villages dotting the Red Sea coastline, many of them did not take too kindly to strangers, and therefore it wasn't always a guarantee that you could resupply along the way. Besides, you never knew if the villages were the homes of the bandits themselves; they would be very eager to liberate you from your stuff if you were lucky, otherwise they would be just as happy to kill you. The funny thing was that they also had a reputation for unrivaled hospitality, if you could manage to be welcomed as a guest.

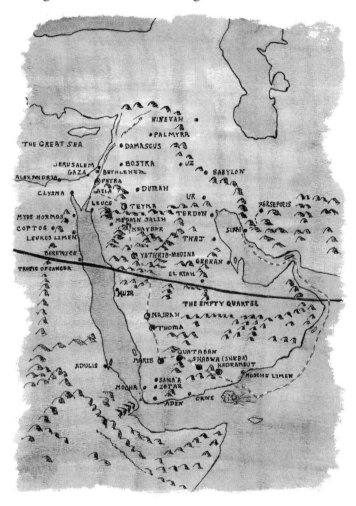

"My men are quite used to traveling these routes from Arabia to Judah. Some of them wear the scars of many battles with those rascal bandits. But I must tell you that all of us must be on guard. Milan, you must make sure that all of your men have sharpened their swords and practiced using them. I assure you that we will be attacked; unfortunately I don't know where or when" Simeon advised.

"We Magi are descendants of The Immortals. We are not afraid of battle, though we are not as skilled as we once were. We are willing to take our chances" replied Milan.

"I am skilled with the sling and the bow. I have killed a pheasant from a hundred paces" I boasted.

Simeon smiled and said, "Ah, a brave warrior indeed. Even a lad can be useful in a fight where every arrow counts."

"I will be glad to dispatch of those rogue bandits. I am not afraid." Little did I know how soon I would be called upon to prove myself in battle.

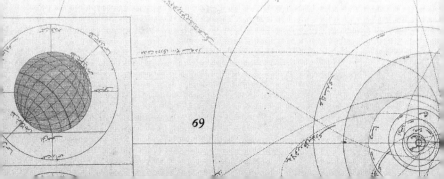

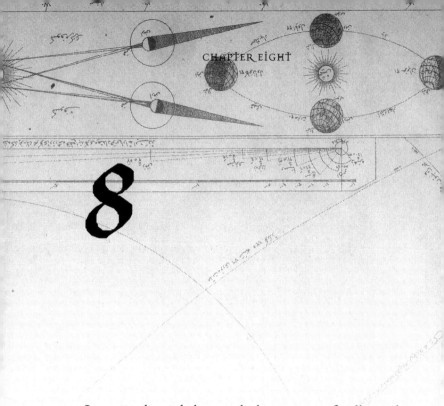

8

It was in the eighth month that we were finally ready to begin the journey. The Magi had collected a trove of various treasures to present to the Messiah. We needed twelve camels to carry the sacks of gold, silver, bronze, precious jewels, different perfumes, various spices, fine cloth and linen, ornate pottery, and of course, the jar of frankincense. We also needed several camels to carry all of the supplies we would need for the journey: tents, blankets, clothes, food, water, and an assortment of medicines, including myrrh, to treat wounds.

When the caravan was fully assembled it stretched

for nearly a stadia. I had never seen such a large group before. There was great fanfare in the city as we readied the camels. The king of the city came to bid us farewell, and the streets were lined with women and children who made a high-pitched shrieking noise to send us off with. And so our next leg began with great pomp and ceremony. world,

We followed the ancient Nabataean trade route through Yemen that took us along the edge of the Empty Quarter of the Arabian Desert before taking us into the mountains running along the western side of Arabia. The heat at that time of year was brutal, and there were times when the shamal winds blow suddenly, kicking up fierce sand storms. The Empty Quarter never had a reputation for being a place friendly to the unprepared or to the weak. It was a most inhospitable place, and entirely uninhabitable. But as hostile a place as it was, the camel was ideally suited for travel across the desert. They may not be the most elegant looking animal in the but nothing is better than a camel for the desert.

By skirting the edge of the Empty Quarter we avoided having to traverse the sand dunes. In some places they towered hundreds of feet above us, making it very difficult to travel. However, the dunes provided ideal hiding places in the valleys, where we could set up camp. Even out here the bandits would have lookouts posted, tracking our movements; no doubt spies had gone ahead of us from the city to report on our caravan loaded with great treasures.

"We will set up camp here for the night." Simeon ordered. "There is an oasis about 3 day's journey from here. Once we reach there we will rest for 2 or 3 days, because our next leg after that will take us through a section of the Empty Quarter."

"As you say, Simeon. You know this area better than anyone else. Remember, though, we must make haste to Jerusalem." Milan ceded.

We set up camp in a wadi (dry riverbed) at the base of a small sand dune, about 150 feet above us. We were only staying here one night, so we did not make our camp very elaborate. The camels were all corralled, with two caravaners assigned to guard them. We slept in several tents that served to protect us from blowing sand at night.

It was difficult to chart the stars out here because of

the blowing sand. No matter which direction I faced, it seemed as if the sand was blowing in my face. I finally gave up and came back to my tent. "Milan, I can hardly see out there. The wind keeps blowing the sand directly in my eyes."

"Don't worry my son. We are well on our way now. I'm not too worried about what the stars are saying to us. We are going to Jerusalem not matter what." replied Milan.

"But Rab-Mag, what if we miss out on something important? What if the stars are communicating something right now?"

"I have spent my life studying the stars. Many nights have come and gone without me being able to read them. But, the signs have already been given for that which generations of Magi have waited for. I am convinced of the validity of our mission, Arcturus. I don't believe the stars will reveal more than they have already told us. I just hope our timing is right, and that we are not already too late to crown the Messiah."

"Will Jerusalem be celebrating his arrival?" I asked.

"Ha, ha!" Milan clapped his hands together and laughed out loud. "I am sure that there will be celebrations the likes we have not seen before."

"Do you think anyone knows we're coming? Why are the Magi needed to crown the Messiah? Can't the High Priest at the Temple do that?"

"My son, I know one thing: the stars have revealed the signs of the Messiah to us. He is the Promised One foretold so long ago by the prophets. Remember the words of Daniel, *'Seven times seventy years is the length of time God has set for freeing your people and your holy city from sin and evil. Sin will be forgiven and eternal justice established, so that the vision and the prophecy will come true, and the holy Temple will be rededicated.'*[27] The length of time has been fulfilled here in our lifetime.

"Even the High Priest knows the prophesies, and he can count just as well as any of us. The Messiah has been sent by God. It is not only our duty to crown the Messiah, but our privilege too."

With that I lay down on my bed to ponder the words Milan had just shared with me. Before long I had drifted off into a deep slumber and so too had the rest of our party.

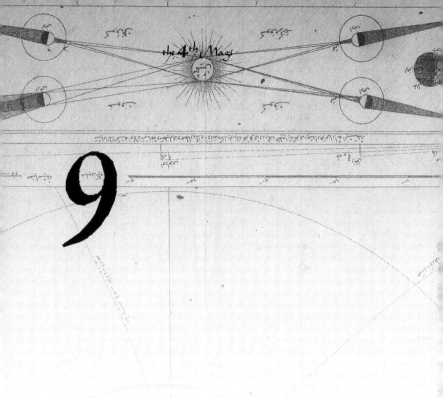

9

We traveled along the seam between the rugged mountains on our left and the equally foreboding desert to our right. The beauty of the Nabataean trade route between Marib and Petra, was that it was a relatively straight course. There were a few towns along the way, but for the most part we had to journey many days between settlements. The longest leg was between Najran and Medina; it took us several days to complete that part. Thankfully, we made it to Medina without any incident, and we were able to rest there for a few days while resupplying for the rest of the trip.

As long and arduous as the journey to Medina was for us, the leg to Petra took us through the very rough and rugged mountains along the Dead Sea. This was where we needed to be most vigilant, because the entire course seemed like a giant ambush site to us. The hardest part for me was trying to remain focused on the purpose our trip. It seemed like such a long time ago that we left Persia, and after enduring a shipwreck, saying goodbye to my best friend, and making it through the heat of the desert I began to wonder if all this was worth it.

"Milan, I am beginning to lose faith in the purpose of our trip. We have gone through so much, and the journey ahead is still quite long. Do you still believe in the coming of the Messiah? I mean, people have been waiting for hundreds of years. Are you sure about the timing?"

"Arcturus, I have never been more certain of anything than this in my life. It has been a long journey for us, and yes, the path ahead is still a long one, but you must not lose faith. The ways of God are mysterious, and as Simeon reminded us back at the beginning, His timing is always perfect."

"It just seems like we'll never get there."

"We will get there, my son. We will get there."

"I wish I shared the same faith you have. I wish Zimri and Kagba were still making this journey with us, instead of laying buried back in Yemen. I wish Badadilma was well enough to continue. And most of all, I wish Shobab was here. I miss him terribly. How can I complete this journey without him?"

"Arcturus, you must understand that there are always costs in anything we do in life. This journey has cost us much already, and may cost us even more. But we must not falter. God will give us the strength to persevere and to endure. Remember the words Moses spoke to Joshua, *'Be strong and take courage.'*[28] We must do the same."

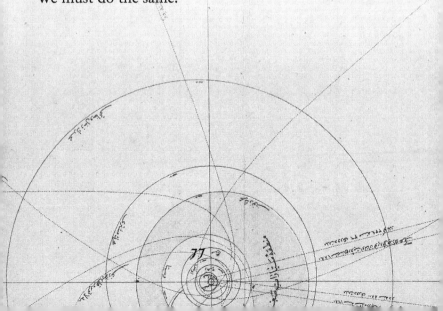

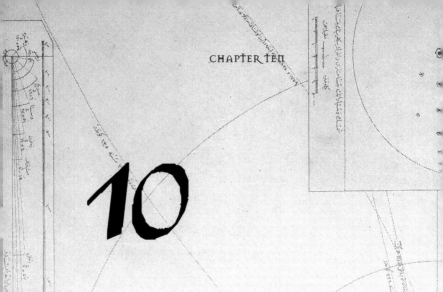

We eventually made it through the Arabian Empty
Quarter and headed into some very rugged terrain.
Though we were not in a sandy desert anymore, it
was now a rocky one.   The mountains towered over
us, while the valleys were rocky and narrow. Here and
there were scraggly bushes and trees, and not much
else. Most of the greenery was on the western side of
the mountains along the Red Sea, but here it was dusty
brown. The sun still beat mercilessly down on us, but
we could occasionally find some shade among the rocks.

The one thing on my mind was trying to avoid

snakes. I have never liked snakes, and I never will. This part of the world was well known for its poisonous snakes, and I didn't want anything to do with one. I'd much rather take my chances in a ring with hungry tigers than to come across a snake. Admittedly, we had just put a few hundred miles behind us without encountering one, and chances were pretty good that we wouldn't see one here; nevertheless I couldn't shake the thought of them.

We had travelled through this rough country for about two and one-half days. The canyon walls seemed to have a life of their own, especially as the sun played off the walls at various parts of the day. The textures and hues of the rock intensified as the day wore on, wearing a vivid red tinge mingled in with the brown ochre. I was fascinated by the formations and would stare up at them while riding my camel. It was while I was gazing at the rock walls that I was suddenly snapped out of my dreaminess by a thunderous roar from above us.

A dislodged boulder was falling from above, and with each bounce on its descent it hit other rocks, creating a landslide of sorts. Rocks were flying all around us, and try as we might to keep the camels under control, it was of no use. They panicked and began to dash hither and yon, braying loudly all the while. Some of our party were knocked off their camels, but I couldn't tell if it was because they were hit with descending rocks, or from being thrown off their camels. I nearly fell off my camel as I leaned back to dodge a rock the size of my fist that whizzed past my head.

It was all over in a matter of seconds, but the damage to our group was great. I gained control of my camel, and calmed it down by talking calmly to it while stroking its neck. I then spun it around to survey the damage. Several of the men in our caravan lay on the ground either dead or dying with blood oozing from different parts of their bodies. Then, to my horror, I saw a couple of the Magi among the dead. I jumped off my camel and ran to tend to Milan who was sitting upright by clearly dazed by what just happened.

"Wha...wha...who…" he said in confusion.

"Master, Master, it's me, Arcturus. Are you okay?"

"Arc...Arc...Arcturus" he mumbled. "My son, what happened?"

"A rock slide. It's bad, Master, very bad. There appears to be many dead and wounded."

"My head, it hurts so badly" Milan said as he reached up with his arms to place his hands on top of his head. When he brought them down they were coated in blood. "I'm bleeding!" he exclaimed.

"Yes, Master. But I think you'll be okay. Are you able to stand up?"

He tried to get up, but quickly sat back down. "I think I'll sit for a few more minutes."

"Okay, I'll go check on the others."

I could see Melchior, Balthasar, and Gaspar further ahead coming back toward where Milan and I were. They were outside of the area where the rock slide occurred and were unharmed. Melchior yelled, "Arcturus, are you okay? Where's Milan?"

"He's here, but he's hurt. He got hit in the head with a rock and he's bleeding" I yelled back. "I think he'll be okay, but he's resting."

Suddenly I heard a whoosh to my right and I saw an arrow sticking out of the ground about three feet away. Then there was another arrow, then another. An ambush! The rock slide was no accident!

When Melchior, and the other two Magi saw what was happening they quickly drew their swords and whirled around to get out of the ambush area. The attackers were coming at us from two different directions, from our front and our rear. While the three Magi engaged the ones to our front, some caravaners at the rear turned to face the attackers coming from behind.

Meanwhile I stood paralyzed, not knowing what to do. Milan wasn't able to get up, but I couldn't just leave him either. My arms and legs just seemed to be like heavy weights, not responding to anything I wanted them to do.

Milan cried out, "Arcturus! Get out of here! Go now!"

I looked at him but couldn't say anything, because I was in such a state of terror. "Arcturus!" Milan cried out again, "Get on your camel now!"

I snapped out of paralysis and mounted the camel. It took a few seconds for it to stand all the way up, but it sensed the danger and immediately took off in the same direction Melchior, Balthasar, and Gaspar had gone. I looked back over my shoulder only to see an arrow strike Milan square in the chest. With a cry, he fell backwards.

"NOOOOOOOO….." I cried out. Then a rage like I had never felt before welled up from deep within me. I reached back and took out my sword and charged forward. I rounded a corner and saw several bandits coming down on their horses from hiding places behind rocks. They had their swords drawn, waving them above their heads as they let out a blood-curdling cry of attack. Melchior, Balthasar, and Gaspar charged straight toward them and met them head on.

It became quickly apparent what a mismatch this was for the bandits. Though they easily outnumbered us three-to-one, their fighting skills were clearly inferior to the Magi's. As I mentioned earlier, the Magi were descendents of "The Immortals" a class of Persian warriors known for their fighting prowess. The fight was on by the time I caught up to my three friends. Though I was better with a sling than with a sword, I still had more skill than these sons of jackals. Their only advantage now was that they were on horses versus our camels, but our perches allowed us to strike down on our opponents as they galloped by.

In short order four of their number lay dead on

the ground, and two more were badly wounded. The others turned and fled.

Gaspar dismounted his camel and walked toward the two wounded bandits saying, "I have a message for your bandit friends."

With that he took a mighty swing and quickly separated one's head from his body. He then walked over to the other and executed the same judgment on him.

We waited for a couple of minutes to see if perhaps there may be a second attack, but none came. We had defeated the bandits, but not before they had exacted a deadly blow to our group. We turned to go back to our companions.

There were a few members of the caravan who made it unscathed, but of the Magi there were only Gaspar, Melchior, Balthasar and me who survived. The bandits who attacked from the rear were successful in capturing several caravaners as well as many camels. Much of the treasure we had originally started out with was gone. All we had left was one camel with an insignificant amount of gold, incense, and myrrh ointment; otherwise we had lost the precious metals and jewels, the cloth, fragrances, and such.

With great sorrow we buried our dead, but my greatest anguish was over the loss of my father and mentor Milan. I wept bitterly and vowed I would seek my revenge on those who had perpetrated this terrible act.

Gaspar was Rab-Mag now. Of all the Magi, Gaspar knew me best, for he was also Shobab's mentor. Both of us had experienced the same sense of loss: Shobab and Rab-Mag Milan.

"Gaspar, I swear with every bone in my body that I will avenge Milan's death."

Gaspar didn't say anything immediately, then he sighed as he said, "Arcturus, I understand how you feel right now. The anger and rage you are experiencing are perfectly normal, but I will tell you that if you hold onto it, it will only eat you from the inside out. There is no benefit to be gained in avenging Milan's death. If indeed the Messiah is who we think he is, then we will leave the vengeance up to him.

"Remember, Milan chose to embark on this journey. He knew full well all of the risks and perils that lay ahead. All of us did. In spite of that, the possibility of crowning the Messiah as King outweighed any of the risks.

"You must choose now which path you will take: one of bitterness and revenge, or one of forgiveness and healing. I cannot make that decision for you. This much I do know, the Messiah waits for us, and Melchior and Balthasar and I are going to see him. What do you wish to do?"

The rage in me seemed to subside with Gaspar's words. It would take time for the wounds in my heart to heal, but I knew Gaspar was right.

"Gaspar, I loved Milan with all my heart. He was my father. He adopted me when I was just a little boy and raised me as his own. I will mourn his loss for a long time, but I too cannot turn away from the quest on which we embarked. I will journey with you to Jerusalem."

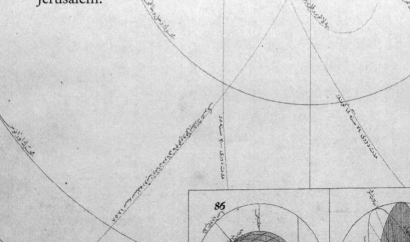

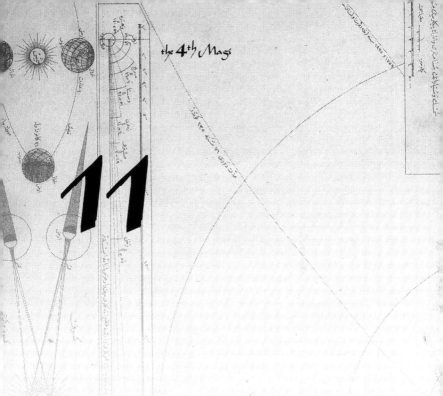

11

The road leading to Jerusalem was busy with all manner of people and animals. It seemed as if the entire country was on the move. Every so often we passed Roman soldiers, standing off to one side looking rather bored, but well equipped to handle any kind of disturbance should one arise. The traffic heading into Jerusalem was so thick that our caravan slowed to a crawl. As we headed toward the city gates we parted ways with the caravan; they journeyed on toward the marketplace while we turned in the direction of Herod's Palace.

I couldn't imagine so many people on the move all at once, which in turn caused me to be curious so I called out to a youth about my age walking alongside my camel.

"Hello there."

"Peace be upon you," he replied.

"Is the road to Jerusalem normally this busy?" I asked.

"Hah! I wish it were. My family's business would be triple what it normally is and we'd be rich beyond measure. No, these people have come from all over to be counted in the census."

"A census? What's a census?"

"Don't you know? Isn't that why you're here? Where are you from that you don't know about the census?" he asked.

"We are Magi from Persia. We have been traveling for months to come and see the Messiah." I replied.

"The Messiah!" he replied incredulously. "Is he here for the census, too?"

"Well, I still don't know what a census is, but whatever it is I don't think he is here for that. We have seen his star in the east and have come to worship him.

How is it that you don't know about the Messiah's coming?"

"Well, I haven't heard anyone talk about his coming, except for the priests in the temple. They've been talking about the Messiah's coming for hundreds of years, though. I can't say I've heard anyone else talk about him as if he really were here. Anyway, if he were here, the Romans would make sure that he participated in the census."

"Would you please tell me what a census is?" I asked again.

"Oh yes, well, um, it's something Caesar has required of the whole world. He has decreed that everyone travel to his or her home town to register and be counted. Evidently Rome has a great desire to know how many people there are in the empire. It must be a slow day there, because they couldn't think of anything better to do," he replied.

"Watch yourself you insolent wretch. I've killed young boys like you for much less," a Roman soldier standing by the side of the road warned menacingly.

"I'm sure you have. But I've dipped my little finger in Roman blood, too," the lad retorted spitefully. He looked back up at me, "They like to talk tough, but they never follow through."

"I don't think I'd want to cross him the wrong way, my friend. The pointy end of his spear looks like it has been used before." I replied.

"Don't worry about him. He can't do anything without the orders of his superior officer. By the time he finds him and comes back, we'll be long gone."

The soldier just snarled and spat at the feet of the lad.

This was not at all what I expected. Milan was certain that Jerusalem would be just as excited about the Messiah as we were, but instead this lad didn't seem to know anything about it. In fact, from what I gathered by the chatter of everyone around me, no one else was looking for him either. I looked down to the right and saw a man walking in front of a donkey carrying a very pregnant woman. "Are you going to Jerusalem for the census, too?" I asked.

He looked up at me wearily, "Actually, we are on our way to Bethlehem to be counted."

"You'd better hurry," I said. "It looks like Rome's count may increase by one pretty soon."

He smiled, then replied, "I wish I could part the traffic like Moses parted the Red Sea, but as you can see we can only go as fast as this."

With that, we parted ways. We turned down the street that led to the Governor's Palace, while the man and his wife continued their journey to Bethlehem.

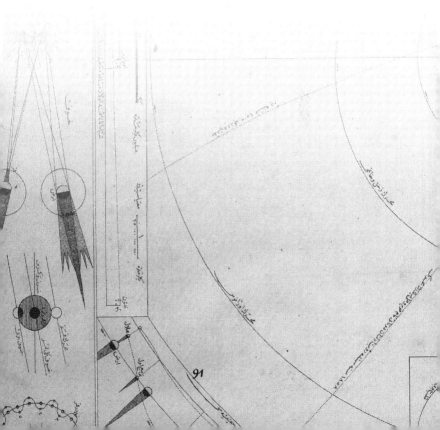

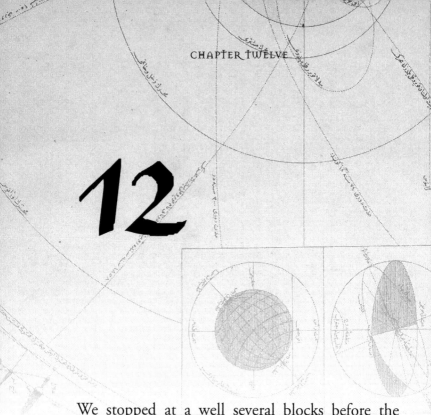

We stopped at a well several blocks before the Palace to refresh ourselves. Not only were we dirty, but our royal robes were packed away and we needed to find them and put them on. We finally found our robes and turbans and prepared ourselves to meet King Herod. We also hired some of the boys who tended the well to wash our camels and re- saddle them with fine blankets and ornaments.

The gate leading into the Governor's Palace was heavily guarded with Roman soldiers. There were twelve soldiers standing guard, with twenty to thirty more off to one side. Evidently the soldiers were prepared for trouble, probably because the Jews were constantly trying to get out from under Rome's boot. Gaspar, Melchior, and Balthasar got off their camels and strode right up to guards.

"Halt!" a guard ordered. "Who are you and what is your business here?"

Melchior spoke, "We are Magi from Persia. We are here to speak to the Governor."

"Magi? I've never heard of you. Go away before I kill you all and feed you to the dogs."

"I insist that we be allowed an audience with him. It is a matter of utmost importance," Melchior insisted.

"I said get out of here. I don't like to repeat myself, and you won't like it either."

Balthasar spoke up, "Fine sir. I can see that you are a man of great importance. You do great service to your king and country, and it is obvious that you are the trustworthy sort, otherwise you wouldn't have such an important duty. We do not seek to cause any trouble, but rather seek an audience with Herod to discuss crowning a king. Do you think Herod would want to know about a king?"

The soldier looked at Gaspar, Melchior, and Balthasar suspiciously. Then he looked at the rest of us even more warily. "Stay here!" he ordered, and then went off to speak to one of his superiors. A minute later the same soldier came back, but accompanied with someone of higher rank. "What did you say you are again?"

Balthasar replied, "Magi. We are from Persia."

The officer spoke up, "Magi you say? I have heard of you. What business do you have with the Governor?"

"It is a matter of great importance. As you probably know, we have a reputation as 'King Makers' and that is precisely what we have come to do."

"King Makers, eh? Herod is already king here. Do you think he will become the next Caesar?" replied the officer.

Balthasar continued respectfully yet forcefully, "My dear Centurion, we Magi are not only King Makers but we are also accorded the same rank and privileges as kings. If you will not allow us to be granted an audience with him, we'll have no choice but to leave. Then you'll have to explain to him how you turned the Magi away from the palace steps." "Wait here. I'll see what I can do." And with that he strode up the stairs into the palace.

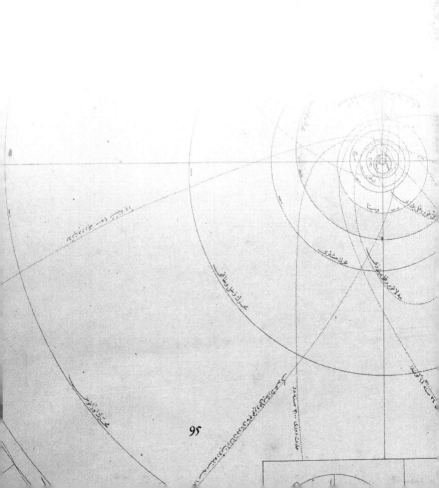

13

It wasn't long before the officer reappeared and escorted us to meet Herod's personal advisor. "I am Crispus, King Herod's trusted advisor." He bowed and continued, "It is an honor for the King to have visitors of such high esteem. You are most welcome here. To what do we owe the pleasure of a visit from the Magi?"

Once again Balthasar responded, "Honorable Crispus, thank you for seeing us. My name is Balthasar, and this is Melchior, and this is Gaspar. Behind me is Arcturus, an apprentice of the Magi." He continued,

"I know you are a man of great importance and have many things to take care of. It is quite important that we see Herod immediately. We are here to crown the new king."

"New king? What new king? There's only Herod, and above him is Caesar. There has been no news of any other king, let alone a new one."

"Crispus, we would not have journeyed hundreds of miles and endured hardship after hardship if we weren't sure there was a new king. We have seen his sign and have come to worship him. Surely you know of him."

Not wanting to sound as if he was caught completely off guard Crispus responded, "It is not our custom to crown new kings until the old one has passed into the next life. Herod is quite well, and there has not been an armed threat by the Jews in several weeks. Furthermore, we Romans only worship Caesar. Nevertheless, I will speak to Herod regarding this matter. In the mean time, please enjoy all the hospitality our palace has to offer." With that he clapped his hands twice to summon a servant. "See to it that our guests are made comfortable." He turned on his heels and departed.

Melchior spoke up, "That's odd. He doesn't seem to know anything of the Messiah. Milan was convinced that all of Jerusalem would be caught up in the excitement. Instead, it seems that we have come at a most inopportune time what with this census going on. It's as if no one here knows of the Messiah's coming."

Gaspar responded, "Well, I can't imagine that Herod would be too keen on welcoming a new king. He is a puppet of Rome, and is therefore bound to honor and obey the wishes of Rome. Perhaps the Jewish leaders haven't advised Herod about the prophecies. I think it would be wise if we were to exercise extreme caution."

The other two Magi nodded in agreement. We sat down and reclined on cushions while the servants tended to us.

It was an hour or so before Crispus returned. "King Herod is ready to see you now."

We followed him into the throne room, a cavernous hall with the throne at the far end. The marble floor was inlaid with onyx in an elaborate pattern. Large pillars held up the enormous ceiling, which in turn was decorated with images of the Roman pantheon of gods. Slaves held up large palm fronds in our honor; but lining the walls at even intervals behind the slaves was a contingent of Roman soldiers.

The throne itself was on a raised platform ten steps up from the floor. A red carpet started from about twenty feet from the platform leading up to the throne. Herod sat on the throne in full regalia; a gold crown upon his head, a scepter in his right hand, a huge signet ring on his left hand, silken robes draped over his shoulders, and fine leather sandals woven with golden thread.

"To what do I owe the pleasure of a visit from the Magi?" inquired Herod. "I must say that this is a great honor you bestow upon me. You are most welcome here. Have you been well taken care of?"

Melchior, Balthasar, and Gaspar stood abreast of each other, and in unison bowed before Herod. They too were wearing their royal robes.

Balthasar replied, "King Herod, your hospitality has been most gracious. We will certainly return to Persia and report how lavishly you honored us. King Phraataces sends his personal greetings to you and asked us to give you these gifts on his behalf." He held up a large bale of purple silk, the finest cloth in all the world.

"King Phraataces is very generous indeed. Please tell him how grateful I am to receive this lovely gift. Also, please take these gifts back to him for me." He held up a sword and shield, both emblazoned with Herod's seal. "I do not often have the pleasure of hosting a delegation from Persia, so this is indeed a pleasure. Please relax, I have arranged a banquet in your honor." He clapped his hands twice, and with that a loud chorus of drums pounded out a rhythmic cadence that ushered in numerous dancers. Trumpets sounded and various other instruments accompanied the dancers. The show was spectacular.

A lavish table was set with all kinds of wondrous food, with fine meat dishes, fresh vegetables, and strong drink to wash it all down. We were so engrossed in all the festivities that we almost forgot the purpose for which we came. The sun had already set, and the star we had followed for so long had taken up its position in the southern sky.

Balthasar finally spoke up, "King Herod, you

have indeed honored us beyond what we deserve. Please accept our gratitude for your fine hospitality. King Phraataces will certainly be pleased with our treatment here. I believe that there will be many more opportunities for great trade between Persia and Judea. But I find it necessary to explain the nature of our visit here. Unfortunately, time is of the essence, and we cannot wait another day to fulfill the purpose for which we came."

"Of course, Balthasar. Please tell me what it is that has brought you these hundreds of miles."

"We are here to ask the whereabouts of the new King of the Jews who has been born. We have seen his star in the east and have come these many miles to worship Him."

A murmur rose up from all those in the great room. It was clear that no one knew anything about the birth of the Messiah, especially King Herod. After a minute or so, King Herod spoke, "A new King? Of the Jews, you say?"

"Yes," Balthasar responded. "We are surprised that you do not know of it."

"I am equally surprised that the Jews have not

told me of this king," Herod responded. "Crispus! Summon the Chief Priest and the Sanhedrin at once!" he ordered.

Crispus turned on his heels and rushed out of the palace in obedience. An awkward silence fell over the room as Herod pondered the news. His face betrayed his anger, although he remained hospitable toward us. "Please forgive me. This news has caught me off guard. I am not sure what to make of it. This would not bode well for the Jews if they have been hiding news of this magnitude from me and from Rome. This is a very dangerous time in Jerusalem with the great number of people arriving here daily for the census. I am certain that the Zealots would try to take advantage of the confusion to attempt some sort of overthrow."

"Your majesty, we did not mean to cause such a stir. It was not the Jews who brought us here, rather it was the sign of the Messiah we saw in the sky. We saw His star many months ago when we were still in Persia. His star still shines, it is what guided us here to Jerusalem." replied Balthasar.

"Star? What star?"

"Come, let me show you." And with that Balthasar

led Herod to the terrace and pointed up in the sky toward Jupiter. "There in the southern sky sits Jupiter."

"Jupiter! You came all this way and caused such a disturbance because of Jupiter?"

"Not just Jupiter, your highness. Rather it was the path it took in the heavens. It behaved in a most unusual way that it immediately caught our attention. I cannot explain all the celestial events that took place without our charts to show you, but suffice it to say, what we saw convinced us to make the trek."

Herod's face softened, and then he began to laugh. "The stars are the stars. How can they lead you to Jerusalem? I am afraid you made this journey in vain."

Just then the Jewish priests and the Council of the Sanhedrin arrived. The High Priest approached King Herod, "Your majesty. You called for us?"

"It may be all for naught. Magi have come from Persia looking for the King of the Jews, the Messiah. They say they saw his star and have come to worship him. What do you know of this?"

The Chief Priest looked puzzled, but then replied, "King Herod, are you plotting some evil scheme to place blame on the Jews? We know of no such thing."

Herod inquired further, "What do you know of the birth of Messiah?"

"The scriptures teach that the Messiah is to come from Bethlehem... *Bethlehem in the land of Judah, you are by no means the least of the leading cities of Judah; for from you will come a leader who will guide my people Israel...*"[29]

"So, has he come?" Herod pressed.

"The Messiah? King Herod, you know that all of Jerusalem longs for the day when we will be free from the shackles of Rome. I will not fall prey to your trickery and admit that the Messiah has come only to have you blame us for some sort of calamity. I am the Chief Priest of the Temple. I am not a stargazer like these Magi. They do not speak for the Jews."

"Thank you for your loyalty," Herod replied sarcastically. "I will have to try harder to trick you next time. Would you please excuse us while I speak further with my guests?"

"You can be sure that whatever these Magi have to say does not concern us in the least bit." And with that the Jews left the room.

Herod then turned toward us. "You are convinced

of the signs of the Messiah?"

"Without a doubt, King Herod." responded Balthasar.

"Very well. I have my doubts about this whole thing, but there is a part of me that is inclined to believe you. So, I will give you the benefit of the doubt. Go to Bethlehem and search for the Messiah. When you have found him come back to me so that I may worship him, too."

With that we were dismissed.

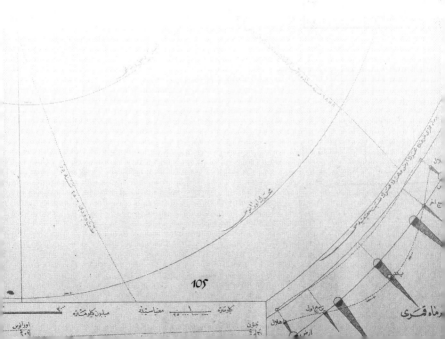

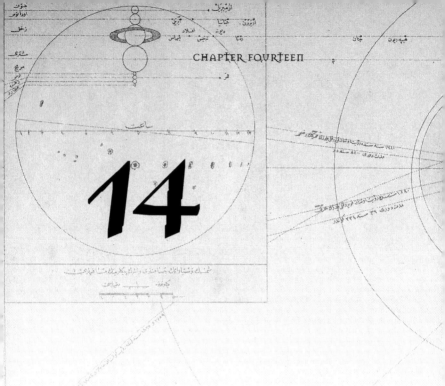

We immediately left Herod's palace, although we were surprised that the king didn't assign guards to accompany us. That was just fine with us, though, as we all had the same impression of the Romans that the Jews had: we hated them. And Herod had treated us kindly, to be sure, but we all felt that he could not be trusted.

The streets of Jerusalem were largely deserted because it was well into the night. It was a short 5-mile trek to Bethlehem, and it was mostly downhill, too, so we made it there pretty quickly. The star we had followed continued to shine brightly, almost seeming to hover over Bethlehem from our vantage point. Balthasar turned to Gaspar and asked, "Brother, how will know where to look for the Messiah? The star only leads us to Bethlehem, but no further. It will take us days to search the town for the right place."

Gaspar didn't respond right away, but after some thought he said, "We have been led thus far, I am certain God will lead us the rest of the way. It may be a pillar of cloud by day and a pillar of fire by night, as God led the Israelites out of Egypt, or it could be by some other sign, but I am sure that we will find the place."

Melchior muttered, "We can only hope."

Bethlehem was mostly dark, although some light leaked out from shuttered windows. There was an occasional torch mounted on a wall to light a street, but nothing more than that. We entered the town from the north and headed for the town square. A few dogs barked to announce our arrival.

"Who's there?" yelled a man from somewhere off to our left. "Are you Jewish or Roman?"

"We are neither, friend. We come in peace. We are

to here to see the Messiah" replied Gaspar.

"There is no Messiah here" the man responded. "Are you one of those zealots? You are not welcome here if you are. You have caused enough trouble for us."

"Friend, we are Magi from Persia. We only seek He who has been born King of the Jews."

"Be gone with you. Magi! Hah! It wasn't enough that we had drunken shepherds disturbing us earlier with loud singing, and now we have Magi. I suppose next we'll have Alexander the Great show up."

Melchior turned to the rest of us and said, "Well. Not even in Bethlehem do people know of the Messiah. How is this possible? Has our journey been in vain?"

Gaspar replied, "Wait. Look over there, toward the west. Do you see that glow? It's right there."

We looked to our left and saw a distinct aura emanating from a few blocks away. It was a strange kind of glow; it seemed to pulsate with different hues of light. Then, right before our very eyes there appeared a column of light that seemed to stretch from the star we had followed to the ground. It was mysterious and beautiful all at the same time.

"What is that?" I asked. "I've never seen a light such as that before. It seems to be a living light."

"Yes, a living light," Gaspar repeated. "Yes, yes, yes. Of course! We must go there at once. We must go to the living light."

With that we spurred our camels on, down the main thoroughfare, and then down a couple of alleyways toward….a stable? The column of light we had seen then a few minutes before faded until all that was left was the light that was pulsating from the other side of the stable walls. We rounded the corner of the alley and saw the gate to the stable swung wide open.

Surrounding the entrance to the manger were twelve shining warriors resting on the hilts of their swords. They shone like the sun, with the light seeming to come from inside their being. Inside the stable were more glowing warriors, they too had their swords drawn upside down, but this time they were kneeling around two figures who in turn were kneeling at the manger.

Directly between us and the manger were about two dozen shepherds, dirty and smelly, but there nonetheless. They looked up as we approached, one of them stood and said, "The angels led you here too?"

"Angels?" Balthasar asked, and then the realization hit us all at the same time.

"Angels!" We cried in unison.

Then, the biggest of the angels stood. He had to have been ten feet tall, and as wide as an ox. "Welcome, Magi. We have been expecting you," he said. "Behold, the Messiah."

There in the manger lay a baby. A baby! In my wildest dreams I didn't expect to see a baby. We had journeyed hundreds of miles and endured many perilous adventures, to come to see a baby. I didn't know whether to laugh or to cry. But then, the mother beckoned us to come closer. Balthasar, Melchior, Gaspar and I all crept closer and knelt as we looked into the manger. And there we beheld the most beautiful baby we had ever seen. I think he was already a few hours old when we arrived, for he was cleaned and wrapped in swaddling clothes.

There was something about this baby that was different than any other I had seen before. His eyes radiated peace and warmth. He seemed to have the same glow as the angels, but at the same time he wasn't glowing. It was as if he was immortal and mortal all in one. I do not know how to describe him other than that. Such joy welled up from deep within me that tears began to flow down my cheeks. I suddenly felt embarrassed by my lack of self-control, but then I saw that the Magi all had tears rolling down their faces too.

"Milan was right," whispered Melchior. "How could I doubt him? He was so right. Oh God, forgive me for my unbelief!"

Balthasar was the most composed of us all, though tears of joy were rolling down his cheeks. "Forgive us sir" he said to the father, "We have come from a distant land to worship the Messiah. We brought some gifts, but I think that they are too feeble for the Messiah."

The father looked up, and I immediately recognized him. He was the man I saw as we entered Jerusalem, the one whose very pregnant wife was riding on a donkey. He smiled and said, "Welcome. God has brought you here along with these shepherds. What you have brought is sufficient. Thank you for coming."

Gaspar ordered, "Arcturus, go back to the camels and retrieve our gifts." I immediately turned in obedience.

I returned with the gifts and handed them to Gaspar, Balthasar, and Melchior. I went to the manger and continued staring at the manger in awe. The Magi took the gifts of the gold we had brought, the jar of frankincense I had picked up in Sheba, and the myrrh from Simeon's caravan and laid them before the baby in the manger. The baby was asleep now.

The mother looked at me and said, "I can't stop staring at him either. He is truly a gift from God."

"He surely is, madam, he surely is. I don't know what to say now. We endured many perils and hardships to be here, the excitement building the whole way. I wondered what the Messiah would look like, and what kind of reception he would have. I wondered if he would already be a man or not. I honestly wasn't expecting a little baby, but now that I've seen him I have such joy and peace like I have never experienced before."

"Yes, the shepherds said the same thing, too" the mother replied, then smiled as she continued, "I never expected to give birth to my baby in a stable either."

"No, I don't suppose you did. But, you know what? Somehow I don't smell the stable at all, instead

I smell a sweet perfume, with an aroma I've never smelled before."

One of the shepherds piped up, "It's the fragrance of the angels. We smelled it too, out in the fields. They appeared to us out of nowhere, we were so afraid we cowered before them. But one of them said to us, *'Be not afraid, for I bring you tidings of good news which will bring great joy to all people. For on this day, in the City of David, Christ the Lord has been born.'*[30] Then a whole army of angels appeared and they sang a glorious song *'Glory to God in the highest, and peace on earth to those with whom he is pleased.'*"[31] He continued, "We immediately jumped up and left our flocks in the field to go and see this of which the angels spoke. They led us here by their glorious light."

I inhaled deeply and drank the whole experience in. I turned to the baby and whispered to him, "Hello little one. My best friend Shobab wanted me to greet you on his behalf. He wanted to be here so badly, but he was gravely wounded on our journey to meet you. I can't wait to tell him all about you." Then I gently stroked his head and leaned over and kissed him on the cheek.

Endnotes

1   Psalm 19:1-6

2   Deuteronomy 18:15-19

3   Genesis 9:26-27; 10

4   Genesis 22:18

5   Genesis 28; 35:10-12; Numbers 24:17

6   ibid

7   2 Samuel 7:12-16; Jeremiah 23:5;
     Psalm 89:3-4

8   Micah 5:2

9   Isaiah 7:14

10   Psalm 110:4

11   Malachi 3:1; Psalm 118:26; Daniel 9:26;
      Zechariah 11:13; Haggai 2:7-9

12   Isaiah 35:5-6

13   Psalm 41:9

14   Zechariah 11:12-13

15   Isaiah 50:6

16   Zechariah 12:10; Isaiah 53:5

17   Isaiah 53:9

18   Psalm 16:10

19   ibid

20   Psalm 68:18

21   Psalm 110:1

22   Psalm 2:7

23   Numbers 24:17 (GNT)

24   Daniel 9:24

25   Micah 5:2

26   June 17, 2 BC beginning at 8:53 p.m. until
the two planets dipped below the horizon at 9:57

p.m. The two planets were in conjunction in the western sky at an azimuth of roughly 290° as viewed from the southern coastline of the Arabian Peninsula.

27   Daniel 9:24-25 (GNT)

28   Deuteronomy 31:7

29   Micah 5:2

30   Luke 2:10-11

31   Luke 2:14

84126428R00065

Made in the USA
Columbia, SC
14 December 2017